Remembering Martha

Jillian, I hope you enjoy Martha - She was a pip!

Jerilynn Henrikson

Cover art by Garrett Briggeman

Also by This Author

Picture Books

Prairie Tales: The Wispers, Grones, and Ponders

Grandma's Prairie Patchwork, A Kansas Colorbook

Ten Little Birds Colorbook

Raccoons in the Corn

Bad Cat!

Desert Dreadfuls

YA Historical Fiction

Teddy, the Ghost Dog of Red Rocks

A Time for Tears

Adult Humorous Memoir

Seven to One

Joe the Gardner Series of Early Readers

No Weeds, No Bugs, No Bunnies

Seeds, Leaves, Roots, and Fruits

Joe and Pam Make Jam

Photo and Poem Collaboration

Seasonings

Illustrated Poem

Dragonfly Water and Skey

Remembering Martha

Jerilynn Jones Henrikson

Meadowlark
PRESS
Emporia, Kansas, USA

Meadowlark Press, LLC
Meadowlarkbookstore.com
PO Box 333, Emporia, KS 66801
Meadowlark Editor: Lindsey Bartlett

Cover art by Garrett Briggeman
www.thebriggemansart.com

Pg. 29 Henry Wadsworth Longfellow's "The Village Blacksmith"
Pg. 43 Henry Wadsworth Longfellow's "The Children's Hour"
(public domain).

This is a work of creative nonfiction. It is the creative work of the author
inspired by interviews with the author's grandmother and other family
members. Where details were lacking the author has used her imagination.

BIOGRAPHY & AUTOBIOGRAPHY / Historical
FICTION / Small Town & Rural
YOUNG ADULT FICTION / Girls & Women

ISBN: 978-1-956578-37-9 (paperback)
ISBN: 978-1-956578-38-6 (ebook)
Library of Congress Control Number: 2023933882

Table of Contents

Opening Aside

I am going to commit a literary sin and begin my story in first person, then switch to third. It's sort of like an actor looking into the camera during the movie and speaking directly to the audience, thus shattering the illusion that what the audience sees is reality and not a made-up work of fiction. I hope you don't mind that I will be writing, sitting here on a bale of brome hay, iPad in my lap, breathing in my favorite mélange of horses, hay, and shavings. I do my best writing here, accompanied by my barn cats, Ringo, George, John, and Paula. I also feel it only fair to warn you that I am what is known in the world of fiction as an unreliable narrator; I just may spin the tale and manipulate it to suit my own ends, and it's up to you to figure out what those ends may be.

So here goes. In the 1980s, during my stay-at-home mom phase (cheaper with four kids than hiring a sitter and teaching), I enrolled in a class titled Women in Literature of the Great Plains, beautifully conceived and taught by June Underwood at Emporia State University in my hometown of Emporia, Kansas. I loved the class, even though I did get a little tired of prairie fires and grasshopper plagues. Nonetheless, Willa Cather captured my heart, and June insisted on making me a better writer by pointing out that the asides and parenthetical remarks in my papers and essay answers were often more relevant than the rest of my ramblings.

The final assignment for the class was to write a fifteen to twenty-page paper based on interviews and/or research about a woman of the plains. I chose to write about my Grandma, Martha Reber Lehnherr, born in 1897 in Neosho Rapids, Kansas. At the time of the interview, Grandma was in her eighties and living near her youngest daughter who agreed to bring her to my house for the day. We were all three excited; Grandma could enjoy a day out, Aunt Evie (who, years later, gave me the litter of Beatle Kittens) got a day off, and I would have the pleasure of seeing them both and, at the same time, pursue my assignment.

Grandma had told me many times that a good housewife always had all her daily chores (laundry, bread baking, bed making, dusting, sweeping) finished by nine o'clock in the morning. Aunt Evelyn dropped her off at my door at about 8:30. Grandma was so proud when she saw sheets on the line behind my house. I didn't have the heart to tell her they had been hanging there for three days. Sometimes I had to rewash and rehang because of bird poop.

Anyway, we had a lovely day. Grandma enjoyed visiting our home on a few acres of Kansas Flint Hills prairie that reminded her of her youth. She was a lively storyteller, and I was a rapt audience. June Underwood loved my paper and submitted it to *The Best of ESU*, an annual anthology of student writing for the university. It was accepted! I am using the resulting paper as a yellowed, dog-eared skeleton to create a fictionalized version of Martha's childhood. Some characters are imagined; most dialogues are my creations.

Molly, my palomino quarter horse mare, hangs her head over the half door, pricks her ears toward me, and listens intently whenever I test the narrative by reading out loud. I hope you like my tale as well as she seems to. So far she has not offered any criticism whatsoever.

Prologue

No place on God's earth cooks up a storm better than the Kansas Prairie. That April day the sun rose high and hot, and a humid haze hung low over the airless grasslands. All afternoon the prairie held its breath. By sundown, bruised clouds piled at the horizon and spilled across the landscape as the sun ducked behind the rolling hills. Suddenly a cold blast of rain-fresh wind whipped blossoms from the apple trees and scattered dust from gardens as it raced from the grasslands into their town.

No orders were needed as the family hurried to make preparation. Young Fred and John, his older brother, urged the chickens into the hen house. Bertha, Marie, and little Martha ran to gather the billowing laundry from the lines. Mama hurried to close and shutter the windows. Papa and Fred rescued the bench from the porch.

They all rushed into the house just as the first fat drops pelted the northwest walls. Almost instantly the metal roof began to ring, hammered by hailstones. Thunder clapped and lightning flashed simultaneously. Soon the violent storm edge passed, and the rain settled into wind-driven waves.

The girls lit lamps and candles against the gloom while Mama laid out the supper: sliced smoked ham, the last of fall's sweet potatoes, and the first of spring's peas. As always, she placed a fruit jar, tonight with a sprig of wild plum plucked during her morning walk. They gathered around the table and, holding hands, bowed heads as Papa said grace. Smiling at each other, they heaved a family sigh of thanks, warm and safe against the storm. After supper, the girls cleared the table, washed and put away dishes, and chattered about neighbors as Papa and John played checkers. Fred practiced his letters on his slate. Martha rocked her homemade rag doll. Heavily pregnant, Mama rested in a chair by the window where she could watch the storm.

An hour or so after they had said their prayers and gone to bed, they were awakened by a sudden rise in the fury of the wind. The pitch of the wind had become an ominous roar. "To cellar!" Papa shouted. They quickly shifted the bed in Mama and Papa's room to access the trapdoor beneath. Down the ladder, into the northwest corner beneath the bedroom, pushing aside a barrel of salt pork and another of dried beans, they huddled with backs against the cool dirt walls. They could feel the little house trembling above them. Boards groaned and windows rattled.

At dawn, they emerged into a perfect morning. A lark sang his gold-throated song from his perch on the front gate. The storm had ripped itself to tatters, leaving white cloud banners streaming against an impossibly blue sky.

As they stepped into the yard, Mama suddenly groaned and dropped to her knees. "Fetch Dr. Morgan," she gasped. "Peter, help me back into the house. The baby is coming!"

The Reber family, surviving one prairie storm, was about to be battered by another even fiercer one.

 *Part I*

Chapter 1
Goodbye, Mama
Neosho Rapids, Kansas: April 23, 1901

Mama lay dying. Martha, the youngest, was only three-going-on-four, and her Mama was dying. Contractions had racked Lena's small frame as she labored to deliver twins. For a day, a night, and another day, her agony had filled the little house. That morning Martha's brothers and sisters, formed a row of white-faced statues on the porch bench of the tiny two-room house with the huge hand-painted SHOE REPAIR sign on the roof. Her father, inside, bent over his cobbler's bench as he ripped the worn sole from a much-mended boot. Martha fled to shelter in the coop with the chickens. Distance and busybody clucking drowned out Mama's misery. Picking up Sally, her favorite Plymouth Rock, and cradling the hen in her arms, she began sobbing into the soft checkered feathers.

At last, the doctor was able to grasp tiny blue feet and deliver a baby girl. She began to squall and kick. After her placenta, the boy child followed, born with necrotic loops of dark intestine coiling outside his body. A second placenta and too much blood followed in an alarming gush.

"Poor little soul never had a chance. Probably dead for at least a week," Dr. Morgan explained as he and the neighbor, Clara Jones, tried to staunch the flow of blood with clean towels. "It is a miracle the girl survives."

Pale from blood loss, exhaustion, and pain, Lena slipped into unconsciousness. Dr. Morgan wrapped the lifeless baby in a towel and placed him in the basin on the washstand.

"Does Lena have a chance?' Clara asked as she washed and swaddled the girl child and tucked her into a waiting cradle.

"I think not," he answered. "Please, Clara, clean up the best you can and tend to the babe. Put her to Lena's breast and see if she will suckle. She seems strong, but first milk may give her a better start. I doubt she will have a second chance to nurse. Now I must go tell Peter that his new son is dead, his wife is dying, and his new daughter and her five siblings will soon be motherless."

Reaching for the knob of the bedroom door, he hesitated a moment to square his shoulders and steel his resolve. "I wish I had stayed with my parents and become a farmer like my mother begged me to do," he stated flatly, and he went to face a scene he had dealt with far too many times.

The sound of the door closing roused Lena. Her eyes fluttered open, and she reached for the baby girl as Clara approached. "Another daughter," Clara said.

Lena drew the baby to her breast and managed a smile as the baby eagerly nursed. "I'm so weak," she whispered. "Is the wetness blood?"

"Yes," Clara answered. The look that passed between them confirmed they both understood the result of the uncontrollable bleeding. "There were twins," she said.

"Where's the other? Boy or girl?"

"A boy," Clara said.

"Did the storm bring this on? Lena asked.

"Oh, I don't think so," Clara responded. "Twins are hard. The girl was first and born feet first. I'm so sorry."

Lena's darting glances settled on the bundle in the wash basin. "Oh no," she sighed, understanding. "Where is Peter? I must talk to him."

"Peter is just in the other room with the children. Dr. Morgan is explaining to them," Clara said.

"I'm so weak. I know what all this blood means. I must speak to Peter now."

Clara hurried to interrupt the doctor. Stricken faces turned to her as she opened the door. "Lena is conscious. She wants Peter."

Peter came to her, knelt beside the low bed, and drew mother and child into his arms. They both sobbed as the baby slept. Lena's perfect oval face seemed to float in his tears. "How I live without you?" he whispered in his halting English.

"You must, for the sake of our children. Please name our new daughter Alverta after my mother, and our poor little boy child Cyrus for my father. No one should be buried without a name. You cannot care for this infant and five other children. Alverta needs a mother. I want you and Dr. Morgan to contact Loretta VanGundy. You know she suffers from losing her new baby. She and her family will love and care for Alverta. They live close and love the Lord. Alverta can still be a part of our family, too."

"Cannot think of this. You ... my heart," he managed to answer.

"Peter, you must remember our children. All of them will need twice the loving when I am gone. Please now, bring them in so I can say goodbye. My strength is going. First ask Clara to come change the towels and straighten the bed. All the blood will frighten them."

On the porch, Peter found all but Martha crying, hugging each other, quietly waiting. "Where be Marta?" he asked.

"She took off about an hour ago," said Bertha, the oldest.

"I'll find her," answered Fred, just a year older than Martha.

"No, I will find," Peter said. "Go. Say goodbye to Mama. I get Marta." Under his breath to himself he muttered, "Why child this way? Why she never where I want, or do what I say?"

Peter was certain he would find Martha among the hens. Whenever she broke a dish, or got a reprimand at church, whenever he was angry with her and switched her legs, she would retreat to the chickens for comfort.

Martha recognized the steps crunching on the narrow gravel path. Papa walked so hard when he was angry. She was prepared for the frowning face that appeared when he opened the top of the Dutch door. The fear and tears in her upturned brown eyes disarmed him. How could he be angry with that small oval reflection of her mother's face? Sometimes he wondered if there was anything of him in Martha at all.

"You come to house, Marta. Mama have twins, boy and girl. Girl live, boy die, and Mama . . . she want say goodbye. Will be hard. You be strong and hear. Now, come." He lifted her and carried the sobbing child back to the house. She clung to him and buried her head beneath his chin. Feeling his arms around her, his scent, his wiry strength, was an experience she could not remember having before. She sensed it was something she would not forget and might not feel again.

Inside the small bedroom, the other children stood at the foot of the bed, waiting for Martha to hear their mother's goodbye. In a trembling voice, Lena told Bertha, "You are the oldest. I expect much from you. See that you cook good meals to feed your family."

To Marie, next in age, she said, "My lovely Marie, you are a good housekeeper. Show your family you love them by helping them to keep clean and tidy."

When John stepped to her bedside, her voice had weakened to a whisper. "John, you are such a good gardener. Help your father feed this family."

To Fred she whispered, "Dear kind, little Fred, you are so bright. Be especially kind to Martha. Help her with her letters and numbers so she will be ready for school and hug her often. All of you, love each other."

Peter carried Martha directly to Lena's bedside. She lay barely breathing, her face as white as the pillowcase. The rusty smell of blood filled the room. Peter knelt, and put Martha down beside her, took her hand, and whispered, "Lena, Marta here say goodbye too."

Martha reached up to touch her mother's face. "Mama, Mama, wake up." She took her mother's other hand and squeezed it as hard as she could. She felt a small answering pressure. Lena's chest rose, and she sighed a long breath. "Please wake up, Mama," Martha whispered. Sobbing, she turned and held out her hand to her father. He turned away from her and left the room. Bertha picked her up. Her small fingers pulled from her mother's hand, and they all returned to the front porch.

Their father was not in sight.

Chapter 2
Rest In Peace

Word of Lena's death traveled quickly in the small community of Neosho Rapids. The following day, friends and neighbors, church members, and families of classmates responded with food and flowers, notes of condolence, and offers of help. With Peter's reluctant permission, Dr. Morgan visited the VanGundy family and repeated Lena's deathbed proposition. Loretta came immediately and claimed Alverta as her own. Peter withdrew to his garden, hoeing and pulling weeds with almost manic force. From the porch, Bertha, Marie, John, and even Fred and Martha greeted visitors and accepted hugs and expressions of sympathy without him.

Inside, Clara Jones and her sister Alma prepared Lena's body for the wake and funeral. Clara said, "She was an angel on earth; now she is one in heaven. We owe it to her to do what we can to make her beautiful." First, they washed the soiled bedding and towels and cleaned the bedroom. Then they fashioned a bier from two chairs and a wide board. They padded the platform with a narrow featherbed made for a cot, then draped it with a fine linen tablecloth Clara brought from home. Clara covered a clean pillow with a case trimmed with tatted lace for Lena's head. Gently they washed her and dressed her in the only nice dress they could find, her wedding dress. The two of them carried her into the main room and placed her on the bier and draped a coverlet embroidered with blue flowers across her torso. Alma closed Lena's eyes, arranged her hair, and placed her hands across her waist. "She is indeed a beautiful angel," the sisters agreed.

Bertha brought in clouds of dainty daisy fleabane from the prairie and placed bouquets of them around and behind the bier. Marie lit candles. The boys brought boughs of cedar to mix with the flowers and help to sweeten the air. Martha came with a wild rosebud to place in Lena's hair. Peter insisted that he himself wash and swaddle Baby Cyrus and place him in his mother's arms. They would be buried together. The scrubbing and cleaning, candles, cedar, and flowers combined to dispel the odor of blood and death.

One neighbor, Lily Johnson, who lived just down the road, was a special friend of Martha's. She sometimes brought gingerbread cookies for the children when she came to buy eggs. Martha's cookie always had braids of dough hanging down like pigtails, just like hers. Lily came that first day and called Martha aside. She had a tape-measure in her pocket. "Martha," she said as she began taking measurements, "I'm going to make you a new dress for the funeral to celebrate your mama's passing into heaven. I know her death is sad for you, but in heaven it is her birthday. What color dress would you like?"

The cloud lifted from Martha's face with a dazzling smile. "Oh, Miss Lily, I just love red! But Papa says, 'No.' He say brown or black."

"Why, yes," Lily said brightly. "I have a piece of goods that will be just the thing: brown with a narrow shiny stripe the same color. I will add a touch of lace around the collar and sleeves. The brown is the exact same color as your eyes!" The next day Lily brought the finished dress.

"So pretty!" Martha clapped her hands. "You sew fast."

"Sewed all night," Lily smiled. She hung the dress from the top of the bedroom door to keep it clean. Martha could not stop staring up at it the whole day long, wishing and wishing the time would pass until she could put it on.

That night, again rain came. All night lightning flashed in the windows and thunder rattled the panes. By morning the rain had settled into a steady drizzle. Clara and Alma came with cinnamon rolls, fried some bacon, and made coffee. Marie helped Martha with the buttons on her new dress and braided her hair into one long braid down her back.

"You look pretty, Martha, so like Mama," Bertha commented. "I wish this rain would stop," she said, checking the window to see if her words had produced the desired effect.

"Heaven is crying too." Marie observed.

With a little smile, Martha said softly, "Mama says heaven is always sunny. Miss Lily said this is Mama's birthday in heaven. Maybe the angels'll make Mama an angel food cake." Her two sisters hugged her and kissed her cheeks.

At nine that morning, a horse-drawn hearse stopped in front of the house. There stood two elegant black horses in shiny black harness, each with a spray of black feathers nodding between its ears. The hearse itself shone with dark wood and polished glass. "Evans Funeral Home and Burial Service" was painted in an arc on both sides. Papa hurried out to the road. "Can't afford!" Peter declared to the driver. "What you do here?"

"Ordered by the boss," the young driver responded, touching the brim of his hat. He was dressed from top to toe in dark green livery. Tipping his top hat and smiling, he continued, "Services paid in full. I'll need some help transferring the deceased into the casket," he added, pointing to the embossed metal box inside the hearse. "Another driver with horse and buggy will be along soon to bring the family to the cemetery."

For once, Peter found himself with neither words nor energy to refuse a generous gesture. He and John and the young man in green moved Lena and little Cyrus into the satin-lined casket. Soon the horse and buggy arrived as promised, and the family, dressed in their Sunday clothes, with Martha at last in her new dress, traveled in comfort to follow their mother and tiny brother to the cemetery on the hill. Clouds lifted and the drizzle stopped. A glowing rainbow arched above them. The April grasses, encouraged by the rain, blanketed the rolling hills in brilliant green, trimmed with daisy fleabane like lace on a spring dress.

The funeral at eleven o'clock that morning was a simple graveside service at the cemetery on the hill above the town. Those gathered recited the Lord's Prayer and the 23rd Psalm and sang "Blessed Be the Tie That Binds." Bertha spoke a few words on behalf of the family. Preacher Palmer delivered a long message about sin and forgiveness. Then he said, "Ashes to ashes and dust to dust," but there were only muddy clods to toss. The family formed a line, with Peter at the head, and accepted condolences and hugs from those attending. After a picnic lunch under the cedars, the mourners dispersed to their homes, and the carriage driver returned the Rebers to their small, sad house.

"What a lovely service," Marie said, wiping her eyes.

"I liked the fried chicken." Fred pointed to the basket of leftovers John was carrying.

Bertha smiled and waved to the boy driving the carriage. Peter went straight to his bench to cut new soles for Joe Camper's worn boots.

"I loved the horses," Martha said. She would remember their large, feathered hooves splashing through the puddles for the rest of her life. And in each heart sat the weight of facing life without their Lena.

Chapter 3
A Home Without Mama

Morning came peeking into the window near Martha's trundle bed. Early rays burnished an auburn glow into her dark hair. She began to rouse, then remembering, squeezed her eyes tight, hoping to shut out the truth. Maybe if she kept sleeping, her mother, not Bertha, would be there frying bacon and sipping coffee when she awakened. Maybe Papa would come to remind her to get up and gather eggs and feed the chickens. Maybe he would not be angry, and the house would not be full of tears.

Marie reached down from the big bed and tousled Martha's hair. "Wake up, sleepy head. Put on your shoes and I'll race you to the outhouse," she said brightly. "We have a busy day ahead."

"Yes," Bertha added as she turned the bacon. This house needs an upset to fit our new family. Us girls are movin' to the bedroom. Papa and the boys'll have this end of the front room for sleepin', and before that, we're giving the whole place a good scrub."

"Where are John and Fred?" Martha asked.

"Fred is out milkin' Wisteria and John is helpin' Papa clean out the keeping-ditch for the sweet potatoes and cabbages. The garden'll be good this year. We'll have plenty of vegetables all winter," Marie explained.

"Mama canned lots of green beans, and tomatoes too. Then her belly got too big to fit at the sink." Martha observed, "And peaches. I LOVE peaches." She dissolved into tears as she remembered how Mama would lift her to the branches where the sweetest peaches grew. "I miss Mama," she sobbed.

"We all do," Bertha said," but we will remember her with love and smiles and thank her every day for all she taught us."

"It's good to cry, too," Marie added, brushing away tears. "Her funeral was just yesterday. The sad is fresh and tears help wash the sad away. Before long, when we think of Mama, there'll be more smiles and not so many tears." She gave Martha a comforting hug.

"Mama's here," Martha said. "When I said goodbye, she didn't talk to me, but she squeezed my hand. Last night, she told me she's my angel."

Everyone was happy with the new arrangement of the house. The bedroom was big enough to allow Martha her own little corner. She no longer had to push the trundle under Bertha and Marie's big bed. She claimed the baby cradle for her own and kept her rag dolls and the two small quilts that Mama had pieced for her there. The girls now had a bureau for their underclothes and a chifferobe for hanging their dresses. The washtub could be set up at the foot of the bed on Saturday nights and each member of the family could take a bath in private. Of course, they still used the same water, taking turns going first. Martha always hated when it was her turn to go first. "Water's too hot!" she protested.

The boys did not mind sleeping on bedrolls in the front room. Rolling up the blankets and stuffing them under Papa's cot made for a quick tidy-up.

The old iron cookstove baked their bread, roasted chickens, and kept them all warm in winter. Against the wall next to it stood a hutch with shelves above for a few plates and serving pieces and below a cupboard for utensils and silverware. On the wall next to the hutch hung Mama's most cherished possession, her mother's cuckoo clock from Switzerland. A table with six chairs fed them, made room for schoolwork, and gave Papa a place to do his bookkeeping. In the center of the table sat Mama's quart jar always with seasonal flowers or leaves. Bertha moved Mama's chair away from its place at the table to a spot near the front window where Mama often placed it when she did her mending. It was just too painful to see the empty chair at mealtimes.

Papa's workbench stood near the front door, handy for customers. A half wall of shelves behind the bench held shoes to be mended and shoes to be picked up. Well-worn tools, smoothed by years of use by Papa's rough hands, hung on pegs on the wall beside the door: awls, needles, waxed threads, various leathers, nails, tacks, and studs. Most importantly, Papa's little hammer, obedient as his children, waited ready to do his bidding. Papa liked the arrangement too. "You can tell he's happy 'cause he didn't say nothing," John observed.

Each of the Reber children had two outfits of clothes, one for everyday wear and one for church on Sunday. One Sunday morning, Martha discovered that her best dress, the one Lily Johnson had sewed for Lena's funeral, had a smudge right in front. She took a wash basin out to the pump, filled it with water, and scrubbed the dress with a little lye soap. After wringing out as much water as she could, she hung it on the line to dry. An hour or so later she went to get it to dress for church and discovered that it was still pretty wet. The day was warm and breezy, so she put the dress on anyway and ran up and down in front of the house to get it dry.

The Sunday school kids sat on benches, and each time someone sat down next to Martha that morning, they promptly got up and moved away. The Sunday school teacher asked why no one sat by Martha. Silence. She asked again. Mabel Lane raised her hand and said, "She's all wet!" The Sunday school teacher sent Martha home, and Papa switched her legs because she got kicked out of Sunday school. As always, Sally the Plymouth Rock hen, sympathized entirely.

Chapter 4
Friends on Main Street

Neosho Rapids was the very first settlement in Lyon County, Kansas, founded in 1854. By 1873, when Lena and Peter Reber began their lives together there after immigrating from Switzerland, "The Rapids" was a flourishing little town with as many as twenty-five businesses. Following Lena's death, sometimes after doing their morning chores and after the big girls and John had left for school, Fred and Martha would walk up Main Street visiting friends along the way. The first stop was always just across the street, where they would check in with Sadie at the telephone office. That morning as she opened the door, Martha said,

"Morning, Sadie."

"What's new?" Fred asked.

"Well, Dr. Morgan ordered an automobile yesterday," Sadie answered. "One of those Model Ts. He'll be selling Old Bones and his buggy soon, I'll bet. Do you s'pose your Papa would buy a horse and buggy?"

"Nope" Fred shook his head. "Papa hates horses. He calls 'em nags. Says they are always gettin' loose an' trompin' tomatoes. And they don't have enough sense to know when to quit eatin' oats. Did you know a horse'll eat itself to death?" Fred and Sadie were always trading interesting information.

"Old Bones's kinda ugly, but he loves when ya pat his nose. There's no money neither," Martha added.

The next stop would be at Kavin's General Store, a block farther down on the other side of Main Street. Sometimes they had a penny to spend. That would buy them each a peppermint or a horehound, and if they had no penny and Mr. Kavin was behind the counter, he would slip them each a candy when his Missus wasn't looking.

Fred loved browsing the stationery corner, admiring fountain pens and charcoal pencils, note pads and drawing paper. Martha liked the fabrics and notions, the satin and grosgrain ribbons, especially the red ones.

"Smells so good in here," Martha said, that morning, inhaling the mingled scents of fresh ground coffee, apple cider, and dried spices. And she always stopped in front of the toy shelf to admire the china dolls. "This one looks kinda like Mama. I would name her Lena," she said.

When they left Kavin's, the next visit would be to Albert Harris. Albert was the town blacksmith and operated the livery stable. Whenever she saw Albert,

Martha remembered her mother reading from the poetry book at bedtime.

> Under a spreading chestnut-tree
> The village smithy stands;
> The smith, a mighty man is he,
> With large and sinewy hands;
> And the muscles of his brawny arms
> Are strong as iron bands.

There *was* a big tree, but it was a cottonwood, not a chestnut. Albert, however, was surely a "mighty man." Mama called him a gentle giant. When they were toddlers, Martha and Fred loved it when he picked them up and tossed them into the air, never fearing for a moment whether those big hands would catch them safely. "Good morning, Little Rebers." He always called them that. "Would you each like to earn a nickel? Strawberry Pony needs a good grooming this morning. Mrs. Kavin has hired her and the sulky to drive out to visit her mother this afternoon, and you know how particular she is. Martha, you brush Strawberry's legs. Fred can handle the rest. Then you both can dust off the cart."

"Do we *both* get a nickel?" Fred asked, impressed by the amount.

"I could buy a ribbon!" Martha exclaimed, clapping her hands.

"Or ten peppermints!" Fred added.

Just then, from the other end of Main Street, they heard Papa whistling them home. "We'll come back before noon," Fred promised. "I bet Papa needs us to take mended shoes to somebody."

"The nickels are right here," said Albert, patting his pocket. "Now get home quick. I don't want Peter Reber mad at me!"

After delivering two dozen eggs to Lily Johnson, Fred and Martha hurried back to the livery stable to groom Strawberry Pony and dust the sulky. "Some ponies are kinda ornery," Fred informed his little sister, "but Strawberry is sweet, just like her name." He haltered the little mare and cross-tied her in the ally-way between the stalls. "Pick the straw out of her mane and tail while I polish the sulky. Then brush the dust off as far up as you can reach, and I'll take care of the rest."

Soon the cart and pony gleamed in the soft light slanting in from the wide door. "Please, Brother," Martha pleaded, "help me on and lead'er around a little."

"Okay," Fred answered, "but if Papa hears of it, we are both switched!"

"If ya do it, I'll give ya my nickel too," Martha promised.

"What about your ribbons?" Fred asked.

"A horse ride's worth a hundred ribbons."

Chapter 5
Cooking

One morning Sadie came to the door with a message from Mrs. VanGundy. She had an errand for Martha. Loretta had baked a couple of mincemeat pies for Old Joe Camper, an elderly farmer and occasional customer of Papa's, who lived a couple of miles west of town. Martha walked the two blocks to the VanGundy house and took the basket of pies from Loretta. Little Alverta stood sucking her thumb, gripping Loretta's skirts.

"Here you are, Martha," said Mrs. VanGundy, handing Martha a covered basket. "Take these out to Joe, and if he is not at home, you and your family can have them for supper."

Martha began her little journey, the hot, fragrant pies in the basket hanging on her arm. Normally such a trip would have taken most of the morning and involved stops to mimic a redbird's call, poke a dung beetle with a stick, or collect leaves from a clump of sumac turning her favorite shade of red for mama's jar on the table. But that day, she dutifully trudged the two miles, slowly opened the iron gate in the fence around Joe's big house, tiptoed up the steps and across the porch, tapped ever so lightly on the door, waited several minutes for Joe to come, slipped back across the porch, down the steps, across the yard, out the gate, and hurried home where the family enjoyed the pies for supper.

Later when Mrs. VanGundy asked Old Joe how he liked the pies, he scratched his old gray head and muttered, "Well I think I was home last Thursday, but I must'a been napping 'cause I just didn't hear Martha knock. I am a little hard of hearing, you know."

By the time Martha started school, Bertha and Marie were no longer living at home. Bertha married George Evans, the cute boy who drove the buggy to Mama's funeral and who eventually inherited the Evans Funeral Home. Marie was working as a live-in housekeeper with the Humphries family, just east of town. At age seven, Martha had become cook, laundress, cleaning lady, and flock manager of Papa's prized Plymouth Rock chickens. He sold hens for three dollars apiece and a good rooster brought six dollars!

Once, in a conversation with Sadie at the telephone office, Martha said, "When hens get old, they go into the stew pot with lots of noodles, except for Sally. She's my only pet. I'd love to have a dog, or a cat, or pony, or a goat, but Papa don't even bother to say no. He just gives me that look. He's not mean," she added. "But us kids know there's no boy's work or girl's work or let Fred do it. It's whoever's work Papa tells ta do it."

One crisp morning late that October, Martha was tardy getting to the chickens. There came a tapping at the door. Martha turned from making breakfast to see who could be calling so early. Sally the hen stood on the porch, cocking up an inquisitive eye. She walked past Martha and went through the front room to the bedroom, entered, and jumped up on Martha's bed. She fluffed out her black and white checkered feathers, sat down, and laid her egg. Sally made this a tradition whenever Martha was late to the chicken coop.

By the time Martha was seven, she was doing all the cooking for the family. She was best at breakfast. Her scrambled, fried, or poached eggs were perfect. Her bacon was always crisp. She could create perfect pancakes, crisp edged and airy in the center. Martha knew all the secrets of chicken and noodles; on Sundays, there were sheets of noodles drying on the tea towel-covered backs of all the dining chairs, while one of those older hens who had stopped laying eggs simmered in a pot on the stove.

In the spring, when the new chicks hatched, Papa picked out the best roosters to raise and sell. The rest of the young males were put into a separate pen to feed out for fryers. It took five or six weeks to raise them to fryer size, about three pounds. Fried chicken was another of Martha's specialties; each piece dipped in buttermilk and dredged in flour, then fried in lard to a golden brown in mama's big old cast iron skillet.

Even so, Martha often felt herself a failure as a cook because she knew nothing about baking: cakes and pies were beyond her understanding. "Drat," she said as she cut a piece of soggy crusted pumpkin pie. "This is awful. Same as the last one I fed to Johnson's dogs. They ate the filling, and left the crust," she complained to Fred.

"Smart dogs," Fred retorted.

"Papa's birthday is next week, and I wanna make him a chocolate cake, like Mama always did," Martha said, ignoring his smart mouth.

"Git some help," he suggested." Ask Sadie."

Next morning, after chores, across the street to the telephone office Martha scurried. "Hello Brown-Eyes," Sadie greeted her young friend.

"I need ta know how ta make a chocolate cake for Papa's birthday!"

"Come back in an hour and I will have a recipe for you," Sadie said, smiling. "Do you have measuring cups and spoons?"

"Nope," answered Martha. "Don't even know what those are."

"Well, I have some old ones you can have. They will make following a recipe easier. You might need Fred or John to help you read the recipe, but if you follow it, you will have a tasty cake for sure." Martha trusted her friend but was not quite sure about her own baking ability, so she called for a little insurance by praying to the Lord for success. The Sunday school teacher had told her class that "the Lord rewards good behavior." So Martha made a deal with the Lord, "Dear Lord, please help me make a good cake for Papa. If ya do, I'll be a good, kind girl, mind Papa, and read Bible verses every night. And I'll leave a big piece for ya in the pie safe on the porch. Look for it Monday after supper. Amen."

Monday's birthday supper of fried chicken, mashed potatoes and cream gravy, green beans with bacon and onions, and that chocolate cake for dessert was a huge success. Marie and Bertha and husband George came, and all were impressed with Martha's cooking. "Bertha taught you well," Marie said beaming at her big and little sisters, "but who taught you to make a cake like this?"

"Sadie and the Lord," Martha answered.

Papa did not comment on the dinner, but he had second helpings of everything, and a smile fluttered on his lips when he took the first bite of his cake.

That night Martha cut a generous piece of the leftover cake and left it on one of their best plates in the pie safe cupboard on the porch for the Lord. When Martha found the cake still there at noon the next day, she figured her deal with the Lord was off, and she, John, and Fred shared it for lunch. She also figured there was no need for any changes in her behavior. There was still one piece left for Papa at supper that night. "Guess the Lord don't like chocolate," Martha mused to herself as Papa savored the last bite.

The next week, Martha made a visit to her friend Lily Johnson for a pie-making lesson. "For an apple pie, you will need to peel, core, and slice six or seven apples, depending on the size of the apples," Lily began. "Put the slices in a big bowl and add three fourths cup of sugar, half a cup of flour, a tablespoon of cinnamon, a pinch of salt, and a tablespoon of vinegar."

"What's the flour for?" Martha asked.

"It mixes with the juices from the apples and makes the filling thick," Lily answered.

"Now for the crust," Lily said. "That's the trickiest part. For a fruit pie, you need a double crust, one for the bottom, one for the top." Lily measured three cups of flour and a teaspoon of salt into a big crock bowl. Then added a cup of lard. "Remember, three parts flour to one part fat, and lard is the best fat! Now cut the fat into the flour with two table knives, crisscrossing the blades, until the mix looks like cornmeal. Then make a little well in the mixture close to the edge of the bowl and put two tablespoons of cold water into the well. Mix the water into the flour mix with a fork. Repeat this all around the bowl in four spots. Now divide the mixture into two balls with your hands. Dust flour on your hands, the bread board, and your rolling pin."

"Now pat the first ball flat, then roll it out with a rolling pin on the bread board with short strokes from the center, making a circle about a fourth inch thick, until it is big enough to cover your pie plate. Fold the circle in half and unfold it into your pie plate. Put in the sliced apples. Dot the top of the apples with butter. Three tablespoons will do. Now roll out the second ball of dough and put it on top of the apples. Next push the tines of a fork flat into the edge to seal the two crusts, trim off the excess crust with a knife, and cut four or five slits in the top crust like a starburst: or you could make the outline of an apple. This allows steam to escape so your pie bakes evenly and the crust doesn't get soggy."

"Bake your pie in a medium hot oven for about an hour. Check it often after about forty minutes to see if it is nicely brown. Also you can tell it's done when the fruit bubbles over a bit. You can also roll out any leftover dough from the trimmings to make little cinnamon cookies by covering the dough with butter, cinnamon, and sugar. Your brothers will love these!"

They each made a pie. "Mine's a mess!" Martha observed.

"Never you mind," Lily stated. "You will get the hang of making it pretty. The first step is to make it taste great, and the first bite will tell you that! Just serve up the slices and watch for the smiles!"

Lily was right. John, Fred, and Papa loved that pie. "The Johnsons' dogs wouldn't turn up their noses at this pie!" Fred mumbled around a big mouthful." And in no time at all, Martha's pies looked as good as they tasted.

Chapter 6
Education

Even though Martha kept busy with cooking, cleaning, and herding hens, before she was old enough to go to school, she never turned down a session with Fred to learn her letters and numbers. True to his promise to their mother, he was a patient teacher. He often brought home beginning readers from school and he and Martha would sit at the table after supper was over and dishes done and pore over the simple texts. One evening they were perusing a book about farm animals. On each page was a charming illustration of a different critter. One featured a beautiful picture of a horse. Under it was the word, "Stallion." Martha sounded out the word. Papa rose suddenly from his bench, marched to the table, and slapped Martha sharply across her face.

"Stallion is evil. Never say this word," he growled.

Martha was stunned. She ran in tears to her room and fell sobbing onto her bed. Fred followed and sat beside her. "I don't know why he hit ya, Martha. I think when Papa was in Switzerland, the neighbors kept a stallion, and he was mean or something. Just don't say it ever again when Papa can hear."

The next year, in September after her sixth birthday, Martha was finally old enough to start school. The little two-room school building stood on Elm, just two blocks east of the smithy on Main Street. Grades one through four met in the little room and grades five through eight, the big kids, met in the big room. Short, plump, pretty Miss Wilson taught the primary grades. Smiles and hugs ruled her classroom. Miss Wilson shared her love for learning about letters, words, numbers, and exotic places. She was also great at handling first aid for scratches and bruises, knowing just how to patch a scratch and blow away the sting. There was always an extra sandwich or two in her lunch box for anyone who "forgot" to bring their lunch.

Ancient, prune-faced Mrs. Prescott, widowed and embittered by the Civil War, ruled the upper grades with two rods; one up her spine and the other in her hand. Earl White, her most frequent target, swore that her Mr. Prescott did not die in the war, "My Grandma White told me that August Prescott had a bad leg from falling off a ladder and could have avoided being drafted, he enlisted to escape. Then he deserted his wife and the Union Army just after the war was over. 'A better choice,' he thought, 'than coming home to go to war all over again!'" Earl, like many of Mrs. Prescott's students, was willing to endure her disposition to get the education they knew she was giving them to go on to high school, and, for a favored few, even college.

Benny Johnson, another target of her wrath, had a different view. "I'd rather shovel shit and hoe corn for the rest of my life than put up with three more years of that mean old bat." He dropped out after three weeks of fifth grade.

Martha loved school, even though she often felt poor in comparison with some other students. "Mabel Lane's so rich," she told Fred on their walk home one day. "She has ribbons ta match every dress, and a different dress ta wear every day. Did you see that red ribbon she had tying up her curls today? I bet it's two yards long if it's a inch. It had *four* loops! I wish I was rich Mabel Lane." Martha felt mighty awful when rich Mabel Lane took sick and died from scarlet fever just before Christmas. She toted a chocolate cake to the Lane home and spent extra time on her bedtime prayers for several weeks after the funeral.

When Martha was in fourth grade, her sister Alverta VanGundy started school. Alverta might have been a person to pity, but in Martha's side, she was a hurtful thorn. In her mind, Alverta's birth had been the cause of their mother's death. Alverta's presence across the room in the first-grade row every day in a freshly pressed dress and newly polished button shoes made Martha's ears ring.

On one occasion, Alverta brought a cinnamon roll in her lunch. She didn't have room for it after eating a ham sandwich and an apple. "Anybody want this?" she asked.

Martha raised her hand. Alverta rose from her chair, minced right past Martha, took one bite out of the roll, and daintily dropped the rest into the waste basket. Perhaps she had not seen Martha's reluctant hand, but it mattered not. Martha never forgot. From that moment on, Alverta became, "That damned Alverta."

With fifth grade came Martha's move to the big room and Mrs. Prescott. It seemed to Martha that dealing with her was a lot like dealing with Papa: do your work, keep your head down, hold your tongue. Most of the time, these strategies worked just fine. Once in a while Martha's irrepressible spirit spilled over and trouble ensued.

Every two years the school was visited by the County Superintendent from Emporia, the county seat. Mrs. Adams was her name, and she was a taller, louder, more officious version of the formidable Mrs. Prescott. For weeks before the visit, the little schoolhouse, both rooms and both outhouses, were scrubbed, polished, and organized. Books on shelves were alphabetized by author and arranged by subject. Floors and desks were waxed. Stoves blacked. Students drilled.

At last the day arrived. In the Little Room, Miss Wilson had arranged a dramatization of "The Children's Hour" by Henry Wadsworth Longfellow. Martha was Laughing Alegra, Alverta played the part of Edith with Golden Hair, and Miss Wilson read the poem.

. . . Do you think, O blue-eyed banditti,
Because you have scaled the wall,
Such an old mustache as I am
Is not a match for you all!

I have you fast in my fortress,
And will not let you depart,
But put you down into the dungeon
In the round-tower of my heart.

And there will I keep you forever,
Yes, forever and a day,
Till the walls shall crumble to ruin,
And molder in dust away! . . .

Miss Wilson read with lots of feeling and ended with a dramatic sigh. The kids just thought it was kind of dumb. Alverta loved being the center of attention. Martha was mortified.

In the upper grades, Mrs. Adams took charge. The tradition was for the superintendent to call on individual students to recite by comparing words. This meant that the instructor would give a student a word or two to use in a sentence. Mrs. Adams called on Martha. Martha stood beside her desk. Mrs. Adams said, "Compare 'goose.'"

Martha blurted the first thing that popped into her head. "Goose, goose, who goosed your goose?" The classroom went from stunned silence to suppressed giggles. The three instructors blushed. A flustered Mrs.

Adams turned to Earl White and said, "Compare the words 'pistol' and 'two.'" Not to be outdone by a fifth grader, Earl scratched his head, and said, "Our next-door neighbors make home brew. They drink till ten and pistol two."

Letters were sent. Parents were visited. No one died. The following year, Earl began high school. In 1914 he graduated with honors in English Literature from the University of Kansas. He went on to earn two advanced degrees and become a distinguished professor at KU.

Chapter 7
Kavins to the Rescue

One morning, as Martha was preparing breakfast, Papa noticed she limped as she brought pancakes to the table. "Come here, Marta," he directed. She hobbled over to his place at the head of the table. "What matters with you foot?" he asked. "Are shoes tight?

"I guess my toes are kinda pinched," she answered.

"I make bigger shoes," he said.

"Oh Papa! Kavin's Store has these new canvas shoes. All the kids have 'em. Can I have a pair, please?"

"I will make shoes. Come stand on paper." He traced around both her feet on pages from an old Montgomery Ward catalog with a wax pencil he used for marking leather. Two weeks later he proudly presented her with a pair of high-topped lace-up spool-heeled horrors. Papa was a good cobbler, but not much of a shoe designer.

For weeks, Martha would head off for school, stop at a culvert over a shallow ditch on Walnut Street, trade the awful new shoes for her old, too small ones hidden there, stow the new ones, and continue to school. On the way home, she would reverse the process. One day on the return trip, one of the new shoes was missing, probably dragged off by a stray dog. Martha, Fred, John, and half the school searched until almost dark. Finally Martha went home to face the wrath of Papa. She told him the absolute truth of what had happened, knowing anything less would just make her punishment worse. Still, he marched her into the yard, directed her to lean against a tree, and whipped her with a willow switch. When he stopped, he said, "You look like you Mama. Why you not act like you Mama?!" The words bit as hard as the switch.

Martha ran down Main Street and collapsed in a sobbing heap on the curb in front of Kavin's Store. Mr. Kavin came out and sat beside her. "Your Papa whip you again, Brown Eyes?" Martha nodded. She told him the whole story between sobs.

"Dry your tears now and come with me." He led her into the store. "Sit here," he directed. He tried a pair of those wonderful canvas shoes on her and gave them to her along with two pairs of socks. "You come here every day after school for an hour to sweep up and run errands. We need extra help at Christmas time. For the first month, you will work off the shoes and socks. After that, I will pay you twenty cents an hour." From that day forward, Martha bought all her own shoes and clothing.

❖

For the Rebers, Christmas was pretty much just another day. Sometimes during the season, the family would walk to the timber along the winding Neosho River to hunt for black walnuts that had dropped after a couple of heavy frosts from the many walnut trees growing along the banks. "Look under the ends of the branches," Martha said. "That's where most'a the nuts drop." The nuts were covered with a spongy green husk. John, Fred, Martha, and Papa would scour the forest floor for the green globes and gather them into flour sacks.

They took their treasures home and spread them across the road in front of the house. "Put 'em in the tire tracks," Martha reminded. "That's where they'll get run over best." As cars and buggies ran over the nuts, the husks would crack and peel off. What was left was the hard nut. Black walnut shells are a challenge to crack, and once cracked, the meat of the nut is difficult to pick from the shell. "I love the way they taste," Fred said. "Can't figure how some people think the taste is too strong."

"I love 'em in nut bread and fudge," Martha added.

"And they make the best ice cream ever," said John.

The three kids would sit in a circle on the floor around Papa's bench as he cracked the nuts with his faithful little hammer. They would pick out the nuts with the curved needles Papa used to mend shoes. Whenever they managed to leverage out a good big piece, they would put it on Papa's knee. He would snatch it and pop it into his mouth. The three of them would poke each other and laugh.

Martha would add the nuts in special Christmas treats for friends and neighbors including the Kavins, Lily Johnson, Sadie the phone operator, Albert the blacksmith, and Dr. Morgan. When they had extra, they would sell them for ten cents a quart.

One evening early in December, Martha came running home after finishing up sweeping the aisles at Kavin's Store. "John! Fred!" she shouted, "There's gonna be a Christmas raffle at Kavin's! Mr. Kavin picked ten things to give away! There's a swell granite roaster, four ten-pound sacks of sugar, two pair of ice skates, a hacksaw, a red wagon, and, best of all, my favorite china doll!"

"How can he afford to just give things away," John asked, skeptically.

"Well," Martha answered, "he has put numbers on each one, and when customers buy stuff, they get a ticket for every dollar they spend. Then on December twenty third, all the ticket stubs will be in a big tub. Mrs. Kavin will draw stubs outta the tub, and whoever has the other half, wins the prize."

"I could sure use that red wagon when we pick up nuts," Fred observed.

"No chance without dollar to spend," grumbled Papa from his workbench.

"I spent some dollars," Martha protested. "I bought some goods for Lily ta make me a new dress and cinnamon for pumpkin pie. I got two chances, and I'm gonna win that doll and name her Lena!" Papa gave her a dark stare, shook his head, and returned to his work, uncharacteristically dismissing her sassy tone.

"Fat chance," sighed John under his breath.

December twenty-third finally arrived, and the drawing concluded. No one had won the doll, so the Kavins decided to put it under the Christmas tree at the church Christmas party with Martha's name on it. Every year at the party, parents brought wrapped presents to be handed out by Santa. The Reber kids, and others whose parents could not afford fancy gifts, got just a bag of hard candy and a few salted peanuts, provided by the Ladies' Aid. When Santa held up that beautifully wrapped present and called, "Martha Reber," she ran up the aisle and vaulted the communion rail to get it. Martha could not believe her eyes when she unwrapped that lovely doll. "Oh, Lena!" she sobbed with joy.

Poor Fred was anguished. One of the church ladies saw his disappointment and quickly grabbed a green vase from the church supply cupboard and wrapped it up for him, a poor substitute for a dreamed-of red wagon. "You must'a done somethin' naughty," Martha observed, "or you would'a got the wagon. You should'a been good like me."

Christmas Day brought fine weather, one of those climatological surprises of the Kansas prairie. After dinner, Fred and Martha went out on the front porch to sit in the warming sun. Martha had wrapped Lena the doll in one of the little quilts and put her to sleep in the cradle. As she sat down next to her brother, Martha sighed, "It sure is too bad you was a naughty boy and Santa gave you a dumb green vase instead of the wagon you wanted." Suddenly Fred jumped up, ran into the house, and latched the door behind him. He snatched Papa's hammer from the work bench, smashed the green vase and then Martha's doll. He replaced the hammer and, returning to his spot next to Martha on the steps, smiling through tears, he said, "Now we are even. Now we can be friends again."

Martha loved that doll. But deep in her heart she knew that her big brother was her closest and best friend. She knew that of all the people in her world, Fred loved her best. She reached over and patted his knee. "Oh Freddie, I'm so sorry. I have been meaner than Papa when he's mad. And if Santa thinks I'm kinder and better than you, he musta not been watchin' very careful. Please, yes. Let's be friends again, now and always."

"Let's bury what's lefta the vase an' the doll in the garden," Fred sniffled, wiping his eyes, "and promise never to fuss again!"

"I promise," she sobbed and practically hugged the air out of him.

Intermission Aside

Hello again. I'm back in the barn. It's quiet and tidy here. My house is a mess of unfolded laundry, undone dishes, and unruly dogs. I have decided I am a lousy housekeeper. But I am a great barn keeper. The problem is the standard: in the house, one must sort, file, dust, mop, sweep, fold, put away, and clean up all dirt; in the barn there are lots of hooks to hang stuff, and one simply removes the shit and leaves the dirt floor.

But on with our tale: here I feel compelled to introduce the Lehnherrs. Now, although both the Reber and Lehnherr families immigrated to Kansas from Switzerland at about the same time, there were vast differences in culture between the two families. The Rebers, you already know: poor, motherless, hardworking, lots of kids.

In contrast to poor, uneducated Peter Reber, who spoke an obscure dialect of German-Swiss, and halting, German-accented English, Alfred Lehnherr, from Bern, Switzerland, graduated university with a law degree and was fluent in seven languages. Brilliant and accomplished, he was also a scoundrel. (Martha would say, "He was a son-of-a-bitch.") He first settled in Florence, Kansas, where he set up a law practice. He frequently drank and gambled. At one point in a card game he cheated a young cowboy out of a whole year's pay.

Before he left Switzerland, Alfred visited one of his favorite law professors. During this visit, he cast lustful eyes upon Ida, the children's tutor and nanny. After settling in Kansas, he sent money for her passage and a marriage proposal. She accepted both.

Alfred went about town bragging on how this beautiful, educated girl was coming to be his bride, arriving next Friday on the train. That young cowboy heard Alfred's boasts and intercepted the train at Strong City. Claiming to be an emissary from Alfred, he kidnapped Ida and hid her in his shack out on the prairie. After two weeks of searching, she was found by the district's marshal.

Alfred and Ida were married. Nine months later, she had a child. They named him Barney Oscar. He had black hair and blue eyes and grew to about five feet five inches. Just eighteen months later, the couple produced another son, Harry. He grew to well over six feet. The two boys grew up without discipline or direction and fought like young bucks, constantly locking horns. Did I mention that the cowboy's name was Shorty, and he was half Kaw Indian? At any rate, I have given you a vivid picture of the stark contrast between these two families.

And now Molly is banging her water bucket. She must need a refill.

Part II

Chapter 1
The Talk

Growing up without Mama left huge gaps in Martha's understanding about sex. Papa was no help, and neither were her brothers. When sister Bertha had a baby and brought him for a visit, Martha said, "Oh Bertie, he's so cute. Where'd you get him?"

Bertha blushed and answered, "I ordered him from the Montgomery Ward catalog."

Fred chimed in, "I think we should get one, too, Martha. He could sleep with John and me, and we could teach him to play basketball when he gets bigger."

After Bertha and the baby left, Fred and Martha ran to the telephone office to borrow the Montgomery Ward catalog from Sadie and sat on the front porch steps with it across their knees poring over the section with all the babies. The cheapest one was $2.25. After returning the catalog to Sadie, they rushed home to count their savings. They were short eighty-five cents.

As they sat there, scratching their heads as to just how to raise the baby fund money, a sharp-dressed grocery drummer came strutting down the street, bound for

Kavin's Store. "Hi kids," he said. "Say, how would you two like to test my latest product?" He pulled a package of sandwich cookies from his satchel and handed them each a sample.

"Wow, these are really great," Fred managed around a mouthful.

"How much do they cost?" Martha crumb-mumbled.

"I can let you have the rest of this package for twenty-five cents," he answered.

Heads together, the two quickly conferenced, reasoning that a baby would be a lot of trouble with dirty diapers and would probably cry at night . . . and the cookies were cheaper. They forgot about ordering a baby and bought the rest of the package of those delicious cookies instead.

A few years after this momentous incident, Martha and one of her seventh-grade classmates, Henry Pine, were teeter-tottering in the schoolyard at recess. Across the street, Mrs Edminston, eight months pregnant, was out sweeping her porch. "Look at that belly," Martha observed. "How could anyone eat so much? Amy used ta be so skinny."

Abruptly Henry stopped the teeter board and gave Martha a good long look. "You're serious, aren't you?" he stated flatly. "You better have a talk with Lily Johnson. Ask her that question. I can't believe that your big sisters haven't told you. Your Papa should have seen to it."

Martha did just that, and finally, she got the facts. Lily made an appointment with Dr. Morgan for her and Martha. When they arrived, Doc had some charts showing male and female reproductive anatomy set up in his office. He proceeded to explain the mechanics. All of them. Martha's brown eyes kept getting bigger. "Is that why the roosters jump on the hens?"

"Yup."

"Is that why all the male dogs in town come to Joe Camper's house to visit his pointer, Lulu? And Joe locks her in the shed?"

"Yes."

"Is that why Papa takes Wisteria to Thompson's bull every spring?"

"Indeed it is."

"For people, there's more to it than just biology," Lily added. "Someday you will meet someone who will make your heart sing; someone who will love you as you love him. Someone you will want to be the Papa for your babies. Your Mama and Papa had this kind of love for each other. This is what I wish for you, Martha."

"Lily is right," Doctor Morgan replied. "And I must add one other thing. I have seen too many women, like your Mama for example, suffer and die from having too many children. Remember that you must have a say in how many babies you have. When your heart starts singing, make sure your head does some thinking and your mouth does some talking. You and the man you love will have some important decisions to make about your family's future. How can you be a good mama to your children if you die because you have too many?"

Martha said, "Thank you both. I wish someone would a had this talk with Mama when she was a girl. She will always be my angel in heaven, but I wish she was here." All three wiped their eyes.

Chapter 2
"I Am No Longer a Child"

After days of hesitation, Martha finally worked up the nerve to state a long-held wish. "Papa, I really want to go to high school.

"No need," he answered, not looking up from his pancakes. "You cook good, keep clean house, raise chicken, make garden, no need." He raised another forkful and added, "Girl not need high school. Lily Johnson ask, you help make rugs. New neighbor, Mrs. Lehnherr want you clean and do laundry."

"But Papa . . ."

"No need high school." His voice was steady. His eyes met hers.

Fred gave her a look that said, "Drop it!"

Martha persisted. "I really want to go!"

Papa laid down his fork. "Get switch!" he hissed between his teeth.

"No, Papa," Martha said calmly. "There will be no more switching. I am no longer a child. As long as I live in your house, I will do what you say, but you will never hit me again!"

And so it happened that at age fifteen, Martha found herself with four jobs: helping at Kavin's Store every weekday morning, looming rugs for Lily Johnson every weekday afternoon, housekeeping for the Lehnherrs all day on Saturdays, and, of course, cooking, cleaning, putting up vegetables, gardening, and herding hens for Papa in her spare time.

The busy routine of her life was a solace for Martha when she lost, next to her brothers, her closest friend. Sally the hen died at twenty of old age. Papa allowed Martha to bury her beneath the lilac bush, one of the old hen's favorite spots to dust her feathers. "She too old to cook," Papa said.

Except for neighbor Lily, Sadie the phone operator, and Sally the chicken, all Martha's friends were boys, the friends of her brothers. Because Papa, out of a determined loyalty to his lost Lena, would never let a woman in the house, local mothers would not allow their little girls to associate with the Rebers as there was no Mama present to supervise. Martha grew up to be direct, blunt, and more than a little crude. No shrinking violet was she. She could not embroider pillowcases or tat lace hankies, but she could stomp a floor-shaking polka or shovel out a chicken coop.

She loved baseball and basketball. She and her brothers even scalped the prairie grasses from a rectangle of ground behind the house to make a basketball court. Lily made Martha a pair of bloomers so she could play too, unencumbered by skirts. While other girls were learning how to hold a teacup, Martha was intercepting passes and scoring layups.

The boys she grew up with were pals, not a boyfriend among them. They thought of her as just one of the gang, but when the Lehnherrs moved with their two handsome sons to Old Joe Camper's holdings near Neosho Rapids, all that changed.

One day as Martha was shelving canned peaches at Kavin's Store, her sister Alverta VanGundy and friend Trudy Jones came to buy fabric for new dresses. As Mrs. Kavin pulled bolts of cloth and unrolled lengths of fabric on the long counter, the two girls were giggling and remarking on the "new boys," who had moved with their parents onto the old Camper homestead. "Have they been in the store yet?" Alverta asked.

"No," Mrs. Kavin sniffed. "Their parents came and stocked up on pantry staples and bought a couple of kitchen chairs. The two of them seem pretty impressed with their own importance, if you ask me."

"Well," Trudy said, "those boys are handsome! Both of them! They look just alike, but one is short, and one is tall. The short one's name is Barney and at the dance last Friday, he took over calling the square dances. He's really good and really cute."

"Yes," Alverta agreed, "but the tall one, Harry, could be a movie star. He reminds me of Douglas Fairbanks."

"Sounds to me as if they are too big for their britches," added Mrs. Kavin as she thumped another bolt of fabric onto the counter.

When Ida Lehnherr let it be known in the area that she was seeking domestic help, several local ladies told her the best person to ask was Sadie, the telephone operator in Neosho Rapids. So Sadie was the one to recommend Martha for the job. And what a fateful recommendation it was.

To say the least, the work relationship began with a rocky start. Ida called Sadie and had her get a message to Martha to begin work on the coming Saturday, and to tell Martha that she would be doing laundry. At the Friday night dance at the high school the night before, Martha was enjoying a bottle of grape pop when one of the dancers happened to bump her elbow as he flew past doing an emphatic polka. She spilled the pop down the front of her dress. Martha decided to take the dress with her to the Lehnherr place the next morning and wash it along with the other dresses and shirts to be laundered.

Fussy Ida Lehnherr, former nanny, enjoyed her position in this new country as a woman of property. When she saw Martha add her dress to the laundry tub, she stiffened. "You most certainly may NOT wash your filthy dress with our laundry!" she fumed at Martha.

"Fine," Martha barked. "Wash your own damned laundry!" Pulling her wet dress from the tub, she slung it over her arm, and walked off the job. She stopped on the way home to pick up some groceries at Kavin's and when she got home, there was Ida, berating Papa on account of his "lazy, disrespectful daughter trying to wash her filthy dress with my laundry."

Papa listened, then said, "Marta not filthy. She clean. She work hard. No need to work for you."

Ida flounced off in a huff. Martha had never been so proud of her Papa. She ran to him and gave him a hug. He stood stiffly for a moment then hugged her back. With Papa, it occurred to her, it could be a long time between hugs.

About two weeks after the wet dress incident, Ida Lehnherr appeared at the door of the shoe repair shop, a pair of worn boots in hand. Behind her, at the curb, waited Alfred with a sleek gelding between the shafts of a stylish surrey. When Peter opened the door, Ida held out the boots and said, "Alfred's boots need new soles."

"Two dollar," Peter stated. "Ready in two days."

She handed him the boots, dropped her arms to her side, motionless, standing, waiting.

From the carriage came an impatient cough.

"My husband has shown me that I was rash in dismissing your daughter because I need help at the farm."

"Not dismiss, she quit." Peter corrected.

"Well I . . . that is, we, wish her to come back."

"You must ask Marta. She no longer a child." A smile tickled his lips. "What you say, Marta?" he called over his shoulder.

Martha came from making up her bed. "I will work for you 'cause I need the work, but only if you apologize and promise to treat me right. I also want two weeks back pay for the days I missed from you dismissin' me."

For as long as she lived, Ida Lehnherr carried a sharp wishbone stuck crosswise in her narrow craw with Martha's name embossed upon it.

Chapter 3
A Rocky Start

Those Lehnherr boys heard their parents, Ida and Alfred, arguing about Martha the Defiant One for several days before they actually met her.

Of course arguing with a lawyer seldom produces a win, but Ida never let that stop her. In their twenty years of marriage, Alfred had threatened to send her back to Switzerland countless times. Of course, she had the advantage of knowing that no other woman in her right mind would put up with him, or their two head-strong sons. Their marriage was more armed truce than happy union.

The Friday before Martha's return to laundry at Lehnherr's, there was another community dance scheduled at the schoolhouse. She had saved enough to have Lily make her a new dress for the occasion. The two of them scanned the Montgomery Ward catalog for design ideas. They came up with a simple maroon twill jumper to be worn with a cream, long-sleeved blouse. Martha planned to wear a narrow red ribbon tied in a bow at the collar. The tailored design flattered Martha's petite figure, plus there was enough flare in the long skirt to allow plenty of movement for a polka or flow in a graceful waltz. The color echoed the auburn highlights in her dark hair and heightened the healthy glow in her cheeks. In this outfit, she blossomed into a beautiful young woman, a startling change from the shabby little girl no one would sit next to in Sunday school, or the basketball player in bloomers.

When she emerged from her room ready for the dance, her brothers grinned at her and applauded. Papa was dumfounded. "Oh, Marta, you are you Mama!" He did not even take notice of the little red bow at her collar.

The young men at the dance that evening were likewise impressed. Their childhood friend, Henry Pine, marched up, winked, made a lavish bow, and requested the first polka. Laughing the two joined the raucous dancers already shaking the floor of the building.

Enter the Lehnherr boys. They had been busy repairing fence the Saturday Martha had stomped off the job. Even though her name had come up in loud discussions between their parents, this was the brothers' first sight of her. They watched, wide-eyed, as she and Henry circled the floor, then stepped up to the laughing friends as the song ended to introduce themselves.

"At last we meet," said Barney, extending his hand to Henry, but taking frequent glances at Martha's glowing face. Turning to Martha, he said, "I am Barney Lehnherr and this is my little brother, Harry. You certainly don't look like my idea of a washer-woman!"

"Could be I'm more than a washer-woman," Martha grinned, noticing the blue eyes and handsome, tanned face, "and your little brother is much more of a Lehnherr. Wow, you must be quicker to the trough," she said to Harry, looking up into his smiling face and vigorously shaking his hand. "This guy is my friend, Henry Pine. He's a good dancer and a great basketball player if ya ever want to get up a game. He's a good shot, but I'm a better passer. Come on, Henry, let's waltz," she said, leading her pal back to the dance floor.

As they whirled away across the floor, the brothers looked at each other amazed. "Well, she's sure one of a kind," remarked Harry.

"Yeah," answered Barney. "Question is, what kind is that?"

"Might be fun finding out," Harry smirked.

"Back off, brother. I saw her first," Barney warned.

As the waltz ended, Barney walked to the little stage at the end of the room mounted the two steps, stood before the three-piece band and hollered, "Find a partner for a square dance!" The accordion player took up the tune to "Oh Johnny" and the dancers found partners and formed two large squares, each with four couples, as Barney began the call. Harry snatched Martha's hand as he claimed her as his partner. The dance began before Martha could object.

Now, you all join hands and circle the ring.
Stop where you are, give your lady a swing.
Then you swing that girl behind you.
Now swing your partner, twirl her round and round,
Then you allemande left with the corner girl,
And do-si-do your own.
Now you all promenade with that sweet corner maid,
Singing "Oh Johnny! Oh Johnny, Oh!"

The two squares circled, and the dancers twirled as they moved from one partner to the next, laughing and singing the words of the last line of the old favorite along with Barney's call. When dancers returned to their original partners, the dance ended. Harry lifted Martha from her feet, swung her high, pulled her to him and kissed her squarely on the lips. When he put her down, she put her hands on his chest, smiled up at him, and kneed him hard in the groin. Then she curtsied and left him writhing on the floor. As Barney helped his trembling brother to his feet, he said, "Well, I guess we know what kind of girl she is. Now tell me, you clumsy jackass, was it fun finding out?"

John and Fred, from the other side of the room, observed the action. "We should do somethin' about those two!" Fred bristled.

"No need," John said flatly. "I do believe Martha can take care of herself."

"Maybe," Fred answered. "But they need watchin'."

Martha rose early the following April Saturday, fed the chickens, fixed oatmeal with raisins for Papa, John, and Fred, and began her walk to the Camper place. She left home just as Mama's old cuckoo clock announced seven that morning. She figured the two-mile walk would get her to work at the Lehnherr farm easily by eight, the agreed-upon time for her to begin the job. She was to work until five, which would get her home in time to fix supper.

A path led along a bend in the Neosho for a quarter mile or so, hugging a stand of mature burr oak, sycamore, and hackberry trees. Scattered redbuds blushed beneath the soaring branches of the larger trees. A woodpecker's drumming echoed from a distance, and three or four male cardinals shouted warnings at each other, claiming nesting sites to attract wives and set up nurseries. Noticing a rich, musky odor floating in the still air, Martha scanned the ground beneath the trees. Sure enough, a crowd of morels lifted their spongy heads, pushing aside the litter of leaves on the forest floor. She flagged the spot with a dead branch to locate the mushrooms on her way home. They would make a quick, tasty supper scramble with fresh eggs and winter onions.

The path along the timber met Camper's Crossing about a mile from the house. Here stretched the open prairie. Three weeks before, landowners had joined together to burn the grasslands. The Lehnherr boys helped with the fire. Barney was smart enough to grasp the importance of this long tradition and to see the benefits. Planned spring fires began eons before, as indigenous bison hunters observed that lightning strikes burning off last summer's thatch, protected the grasses from invading trees, and attracted bison to the lush new growth. Now fenced Hereford cattle grazed where massive herds of migrating bison once roamed.

Martha paused for a moment, shading her eyes as the morning sun lit up the rolling green expanse from the far eastern horizon. To the west, Old Joe's two-story stone house snuggled into the hillside at the end of a winding lane. The sun lit the simple white limestone façade. "The house of my dreams," Martha thought to herself. "Old Joe has earned his rest, and now it's full'a Lehnherrs. Well, Barney's not so bad, and at least, I get paid to keep it clean!" She trudged uphill toward the house.

At just that moment, Barney woke from a vivid dream of petite Martha Reber whopping his brother over the head with a gigantic wooden spoon. He woke up laughing, stretched, yawned, rolled out of bed, and, as was his ritual, stepped to his east window to check on the morning. And there, head down, silhouetted against the rising sun, this girl from his dreams marched up the hill toward her day of work. "She walks like a man, dances like a demon, and fights dirty. And I think I'm in love," he said to himself and hurried to get dressed to meet her at the door.

As Barney grabbed his clothes, his mind ticked off obstacles to a match with Martha. Pulling on his blue chambray work shirt, he mumbled to himself, "Mother hates her." Stuffing his legs into canvas pants, he added, "Harry just wants to use her like every pretty girl he meets, and she's smart enough to see it." Bending over to find his boots under the bed, he said, "Father, the shyster, will show his true stripes. I think her pop already has him figured out and probably thinks I'm just like my old man. And I'm sure her brothers figure I'm just a smaller Harry." Rummaging in the dresser for a belt, he mused, "I'm almost twenty and she's barely sixteen. I have no money of my own. I know a little about farming and not much else." Finally dressed, he eyed himself in the mirror over the dresser and said, "But I know I'm smart, good at figuring things out, and I'm strong and healthy."

He could feel his heart swell with admiration for this unlikely, gutsy, profane, beautiful little woman. "Now, I just have to convince her to like me back," he informed his reflection in the dresser mirror.

Chapter 4
An Unlikely Love Song

Martha started in surprise when Barney jerked the door open at her first knock. "Sorry, I didn't mean to scare you," he blurted. "I saw you coming. Come on in."

"Is your Mama fixin' breakfast?" She remarked, cautiously stepping into the quiet house.

"No, Mother and Father have taken the train to Kansas City. Father has business there and Mother wanted to do some real shopping, as she puts it. Harry is upstairs sleeping off a late night in Emporia. Mother left you a list," he said, handing her a note.

"I don't think Papa would like me workin' without her here," she said, nervously taking a step back and stuffing her hands into the pockets of her apron.

"Tell you what," he said quietly. "I'll help you with that list. We can finish by noon, and you can leave before Harry wakes up. I promise I will behave and do just what you tell me. First on the list is laundry. Did you bring any filthy dresses to add to the tub?"

"No, Mr. Lehnherr, I didn't." She returned his teasing smile. "That list is long. We best git to it!"

They spent the morning working side by side. He kept the wash boiler hot while she scrubbed clothes on the washboard. She rinsed and he wrung. They each filled a line to dry. She showed him how to hang shirts by the tails, not the shoulders, and pants by the waist not the cuffs. They went to the house, and he swept and mopped while she dusted. Then together they returned to take the sun-scented clothing from the lines, folding it into baskets to take into the house and put away: linens into the press, dresses and shirts to the kitchen to sprinkle and iron with small, heavy irons heated on the cookstove. Barney carried the ironed dresses, shirts, and pants to be hung in chifferobes or to place, folded, into drawers. He quietly left Harry's clothes stacked by his bedroom door. As Barney predicted, they finished by noon.

From the tap in the springhouse built into the hill behind the main house, they each drank long from the tin cup on a convenient hook. "I'm starving." Barney said. "Let's make a picnic and stop by the woods on your way home. I'll walk you as far as the river. We have plenty of time. Your Papa won't be expecting you until late afternoon."

Martha gave him a long, steady look. He knew this was an important moment. He took her hand and said, "I promise you can trust me. I want us to be friends."

"Okay," she replied. "Friends it is! What you got to make a picnic?"

"Roast beef sandwiches, sweet pickles, and an apple?"

"Perfect," she said. "And a couple a jars of that spring water. It tastes wonderful. And you can help me pick some morels I saw on the way here. Papa loves 'em scrambled with eggs." Barney took last night's leftover roast from the cooling box in the stream that ran through the northwest corner of the spring house. They hurried back inside to the kitchen to make their picnic.

With Barney carrying the picnic basket, walking side by side, they retraced Martha's steps from the sunrise. They paused in their walk when they reached the branch Martha had stuck in the loamy earth to mark the morels earlier that morning. It took them only a few minutes to gather a pound or so of the tasty fungi and bundle them into her apron.

There in the shade of the river trees, they chose a fallen oak log where they sat to enjoy the picnic and each other's company. "Let's keep our morning of work between the two of us," Barney said. "I don't want there to be any question about you getting your full pay."

"Okay," Martha answered, "but you gotta let me pay you back for half a day's work."

"How about saving the first two waltzes for me at the dance this Friday?"

"We'll see," she answered and surprised herself by blushing.

Noticing her glowing cheeks, and smiling his most dazzling smile, he took her hand, kissed it lightly, stood, and turned to begin his walk home, whistling "Oh, Johnny" as he strode along. She picked up her bundle of mushrooms and began walking away from him, back toward town, humming that same jaunty tune to herself.

Glancing back once, she caught him looking at her from a distance. Still whistling, he waved. She waved back, a big wave, up on her tiptoes, smiling. She set her bundle down and waved with both arms above her head. Picking up her mushrooms and turning toward home again, surprised, she whispered to herself, "I do believe my heart's a-singing."

The End
(or perhaps just the beginning)

A Final Aside

I just sang "Oh, Johnny" to the Beatle Cats. They are the only audience tolerant of my singing voice. Molly is saddled and standing patiently in the crossties. Both of us are looking forward to an easy canter through the unfenced meadow of bluestem grass across the road. She is a dream to ride, smoother than a rocking chair. Starting from a standstill, she will pick up a lope in whichever lead I cue, in one stride.

Here I end my story because this is where Grandma Martha ended her tale about her childhood that day we spent talking. Also this is where I feel like stopping. It fits my purpose and seems right. Of course there is much more to her story. In spite of objections from both families, she and Barney were married a few months after that sweet picnic in the woods.

Martha did share with me during the interview, that she and Barney eloped by train to Emporia for a quick ceremony at the courthouse in late fall a few months after they first met at the community dance at the schoolhouse. When they returned to The Rapids that snowy November day, as the train chugged away eastward, he turned to her and asked, "Do you have any money?" She fished in her purse and found a few coins. "Can I have it, Honey?" he asked. She handed the coins to him. He reached into his pocket, pulled out some change, and put all the coins into his right hand. He then reared back and pitched it all as far as he could into the snow. "We might as well start with nothing," he said.

At this point in her tale, Martha laughed. "You can't imagine how many times I went back to the railroad yard, lookin' for that handful of change!"

She also shared that on their fifth wedding anniversary, Grandpa surprised her with a life-long dream, an elegant black Morgan gelding, broke to ride or drive. She named him Oh Johnny because, as she always said, "That was the song Barney taught my heart to sing."

Martha had a special spirit that won her many friends as a child and all through her years. This gift allowed her to enjoy life and see humor where many would find none.

As an adult, she spurned the drabness of all those brown dresses by wearing a red one whenever possible. One of the joys of adulthood was going to a dance or out to dinner decked out in a red outfit and a couple of pounds of costume jewelry. Her kind, generous nature earned her many friends. She eagerly welcomed many to her table and was always present in times of need with food in hand and a smile in her brown eyes.

No visitor ever left her home empty-handed.

As I look back on her childhood stories, compare them to my own, and think of how we raised our own kids, I can't help wondering if having too much might be more trouble than having too little. I guess in any generation, all you can do is the best you can do.

And so here we are at the end. My heart is full of other memories: of Grandma and Grandpa, of aunts, uncles, and cousins; joys and sorrows; tears and laughter. Will there be more chapters to write? Who knows? I'm nearly eighty now myself, and the clock is ticking. Perhaps the next stories will be penned by someone farther down on a branch in the family tree. From the middle limbs, looking down, I'm seeing hints among the lower twigs and leaves that this may be true.

Molly and I have a glorious pass through ripened bluestem and sunflowers. Now in late summer, her coat echoes their golden glow. We stop and I break off a few sunflowers to put in the fruit jar that is always in the middle of my kitchen table.

We agree to pause looking west to watch the finale of today's prairie sunset. Just enough mare's tail clouds provide a perfect backdrop for the day's last act. Martha's favorite shade of red dominates the cast of characters tonight, upstaging hues of orange, pink and lavender. As the curtain falls, night's stars crowd the stage until sunrise.

We cross the road and head for the barn. Home now, Molly nickers for oats. I know how she feels. I'm hankering for a piece of that apple pie I left cooling in Great Grandma Lena's old pie safe. Grandma Martha taught me how to make apple pie, both pretty and delicious. Stop in for a slice. My Grandma also taught me to love sharing.

Thanks for reading,
Now it's really
The End.

Postscript

Immersed in this project, I couldn't resist asking for input from any of my nineteen first cousins, and my sister, if they would care to include some memories of our Grandmother. Here's a few:

- My own favorite is of the 50-S Drive-in Theater. When Grandma and Grandpa Lehnherr lived at Lake Kahola, they would go to the Drive-in every time the show changed. This involved an eighteen-mile drive, usually with a backseat full of sweaty grandkids. We kids would spend most of the duration of the movie going to the snack bar up front or taking advantage of the playground next to it. When the movie was over, we would pile back into that narrow backseat and Grandpa would steer into the exit parade. As he drove off, Grandma would always say, "Well, that show was sure not what I expected it would be!"

- From my sister, Mary Beth McCreary: "I can remember one summer when I was taking a French class at ESU. After class I'd walk down to the old Guy's Shop building where Grandma worked at the drycleaner shop. I'd stop at Willards and get glazed donuts and two 7ups. Then we'd watch *As the World Turns* together. This was special because I had Grandma all to myself. Usually I had to share with all the cousins."

- My cousin Pam Gull also remembers an *As the World Turns* story: "One day my Mom, Betty, and Grandma were watching ATWT, and Peter Bogdonovitch, who played Jeff, was wanting to be released from the show to go on to bigger and better things, (He was most famous for directing *The Last Picture Show* and discovering Cybill Shepherd) so the writers deleted him out of the show by killing off his character. The women were so upset that they called the welding shop, sobbing that 'Jeff died.' Grandpa and my dad responded, 'Who the hell is Jeff?' and were sure their women folk were nuts for being upset about the death of a TV character!"

- Cousin Mike Powell: "She always met us at the door in her muumuu. When we left, she always waved until we were out of sight. While visiting, she might come up with a fake cough and say, 'I think I need a little nip of my wine.' (Mogen David) Once when I cut my own hair, Grandma tried to cover the bald spots with shoe polish. Mom spotted it right away."

- I was always impressed that she could down a sixteen ounce Coke in one tip. Grandpa claimed she had "a cast iron gullet."

- All of us enjoyed the cheap candy and cookies she bought at the Kress: maple chews, marshmallow cremes, wafer cookies (fish food), and chocolate covered cherries!
- When I was small, I loved riding the dust mop when she swirled it around the linoleum floor to polish after waxing.
- Cousin Wayne Noller mentioned that she brought Polly the parrot home from the dry cleaners where she worked, and Grandpa Barney promptly taught the bird to swear.
- She never returned from shopping without opening her purse and counting her money.

As my sister, Mary Beth, is fond of saying, "She was a pip!"

Now that I think of it, that pip thing seems to run in the family, especially among the women.

Acknowledgments

As always, the first to thank is my dear partner of sixty years, Duane Henrikson. He keeps my feet grounded and my computer on task.

I also appreciate the support for my work of a bunch of friends, some next door or around the corner, and some discovered or rediscovered on Facebook.

The Emporia Writers Group is an unfailing source of inspiration, appreciation, and fun.

Thanks to Marcia Lawrence for a thoughtful early edit and a pot of pesto.

Thanks to Carmaine Ternes for steadfast support of my efforts and excellent suggestions to improve my narrative.

My dear friend Jean-Ellen Kegler, eager to do a read-through, offered enthusiastic support and caught some elusive edits. Thanks to her also for polishing and helping to make it "golden."

Thanks to June Underwood for the inspiration to write Martha's story and for her enthusiastic reaction to a recent draft.

Thanks to Sharon Stephens for wading through the thing with red pen in hand, listening to the latest snippets, and for being a wise, steadfast, and funny friend.

About the Author

Jerilynn Jones Henrikson has spent her life in Emporia, Kansas, which she considers her front porch to the rolling Flint Hills and expansive skies of East Central Kansas. Here she and her veterinarian husband Duane have raised four kids, who also love being half way to everywhere. Jerilynn has loved teaching English, collecting friends, and telling tales. *Remembering Martha* is her favorite, so far.

Books are a way to explore, connect, and discover. Reading gives us the gift of living lives and gaining experiences beyond our own. Publishing books is our way of saying—

We love these words,
we want to play a role in preserving them,
and we want to help share them with the world.

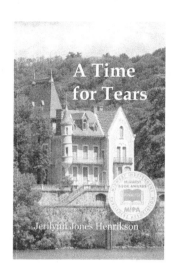

Set in World War II, *A Time for Tears* by Jerilyn Jones Henrikson examines three people (Andre from Soissons, France; Daniel from Topeka, Kansas; and Rachel from Paris) who are caught in a tangle of events and emotions.

Andre Jabot, a teenage French aristocrat, is enraged by the killing of his young brother as the Nazis blitz the nearby village of Soissons. He swears vengeance and finds his way to England to join De Gaulle and the Resistance. Daniel Hagelman, a young Jewish grocer from Kansas, cannot turn his back on the horror of Hitler's Nazis and travels to England to volunteer in the Royal Air Force, leaving behind a wife and newborn baby girl. Fifteen-year-old Rachel Ropfogel's parents, upper class Parisian Jews, see the oncoming disaster as France falls to the Nazis. They arrange sanctuary for their daughter in the remote village of Le Chambon-sur-Lignon where she assumes a new identity, Simon Bouret, a twenty-year-old art teacher.

—Midwest Book Review